T☢XIC

❝ 'You are all wrong!' said Tyler in a loud, clear voice.

Everyone fell silent.

'The kidnappers do not come from another village. They come from under the sea.' ❞

THE
BATTLE
OF THE
UNDERSEA
KINGDOM

The Battle of the Undersea Kingdom
by Jonny Zucker
Illustrated by Alan Brown

Published by Ransom Publishing Ltd.
Radley House, 8 St. Cross Road, Winchester, Hampshire
SO23 9HX, UK
www.ransom.co.uk

ISBN   978 178127 710 2
First published in 2015

A CIP catalogue record of this book is available from the British Library.

THE BATTLE OF THE UNDERSEA KINGDOM

JONNY ZUCKER

ILLUSTRATED BY

ALAN BROWN

Ransom

Chapter 1

'The mayor has been kidnapped!' screeched an elderly woman, as she ran into the sea-front boat repair shop.

Danny and his dad, Tyler, looked up from the boat they were fixing and followed the woman out of the shop.

It was dusk, and the sleepy little village of Tidehaven should have been quiet.

But now everyone was gathered in the village square.

A village elder called Caleb was holding up a piece of paper.

'We found this ransom note,' he explained. 'It says we will only get the mayor back if we pay a hundred gold coins to his kidnappers.'

'Where was the note found?' shouted someone.

'On the beach,' replied Caleb.

'The kidnappers must come from a nearby village,' said someone else.

'They want the money to be left on the rocks, by the sand dunes at the top end of the village,' said Caleb.

'Which village do you think did it?' asked someone.

'You are all wrong!' said Tyler in a loud, clear voice.

Everyone fell silent.

'The kidnappers do not come from another village. They come from under the sea.'

'This is no time for your silly sea stories, Tyler,' said Caleb wearily.

Everybody knew about Tyler and his strange stories about creatures under the sea.

Nobody took him seriously – they all just thought he was a bit odd.

'The note was found on the beach,' continued Tyler. 'The ransom money is to be left near the sand dunes. Sea creatures are the kidnappers – it's obvious.'

But Tyler was shouted down. The villagers ignored him and carried on talking about other villages.

Tyler and Danny listened to the other villagers for a while. Then they returned to their repair shop.

'Get some sleep son,' said Tyler. 'We have much work to do.'

Danny nodded. He didn't know if his dad's stories about creatures under the sea were true or not, and he had no idea what his dad was planning.

But there was no way he was going to miss it.

CHAPTER 2

'Psst. Danny.'

Danny opened his eyes and saw Tyler leaning over his bed. The wall clock said 5 a.m.

'What's going on?' mumbled Danny.

'We're going to look for the mayor,' said Tyler. 'But we need to move fast.'

*****

Snatching some apples for breakfast, they crept out of the house and hurried down the quiet village lane.

A few minutes later they reached Able Beach. Producing a key, Tyler opened a large metal shack. Between them they pulled out a small wooden boat called *Pride* and a stack of diving equipment.

'Are you sure about this?' asked Danny.

'I've seen figures under the water on several occasions,' replied Tyler. 'When I was a lad I was always told that these creatures were a rough, aggressive people. I'm sure that they will have taken the mayor.'

Danny shrugged his shoulders and helped Tyler put all of the gear inside the boat.

True or not, thought Danny, *it's an adventure.*

Then they slid the boat gently into the water and clambered in.

Tyler did the rowing. The water was very calm.

'OK,' said Tyler, when they were about a mile out. 'This is the area where I've seen the creatures over the years. We'll need to be on our guard though. If they see us, they'll attack us.'

It took them fifteen minutes to change into their wetsuits and get their diving equipment ready.

Tyler gave Danny a thumbs-up and, like two sleek dolphins, they leaned over the side of the boat and dropped below the water line.

CHAPTER 3

Danny had been diving since he was eight. He knew what he was doing.

So he and Tyler swam smoothly towards the sea bed, side by side.

They had enough oxygen to last for an hour, which would give them a decent window of time to search for the mayor.

They passed some orange coral, a shoal of light blue fish and several sea caves.

Danny was pretty sure he believed his dad's tales about seeing various sea creatures over the years, but there was a little patch of doubt in his mind.

What if Tyler had imagined them? Was his dad as crazy as some people thought he was?

Further and further down they went, passing purple sea plants and huge red fish with vicious-looking teeth.

They had just exchanged a nod and a wave to show that all was OK, when they entered a dark swirling mist.

It became very hard to see, but they stuck closely together.

After swimming for another fifty metres or so, the mist began to lift.

But just as they began to emerge from the swirl, they heard a loud clapping sound. A second later, something large smacked into both of them and sent them spinning out of control.

CHAPTER 4

Danny crashed backwards and banged his diving helmet against a large blue rock.

He was stunned, but luckily his helmet wasn't damaged.

Before he could recover, Danny was thwacked again. But this time, as he looked around, he saw what had hit him.

It was the tail of a furious-looking green and blue merman.

So Tyler was right – there *were* creatures under the sea! And they seemed to be dangerous.

Over the merman's shoulder, Danny could see Tyler being attacked by another merman.

The merman went to hit Danny again, but this time Danny was ready. He darted out of the way and shoved him hard.

The merman reeled backwards. With a furious look on his face he powered back towards Danny. Danny caught his tail and swung it round, finally letting go with as much power as he could muster.

The merman yelped in pain, swam speedily over to his friend and yanked him away from Tyler.

The two mermen then swam away at great speed. In a few moments they were gone.

Tyler swam over to Danny.

'Are you OK?' he mouthed through his helmet.

Danny nodded, although he was badly shaken. The attack had been violent and unprovoked.

These mermen must be the ones who had kidnapped the mayor. Why else would they attack Danny and Tyler?

'These are the creatures I've seen before.' indicated Tyler. 'Do you want to go back?' he asked, pointing up to the surface.

Danny shook his head, although a ripple of fear swept through him.

Tyler gave him a squeeze on the shoulder and they set off once again, this time swimming in the direction the mermen had taken.

They swam in silence for a while, until Danny held up his hand for them both to the stop.

In the distance he could see a tall archway.

And he was pretty sure he knew what it was.

It looked like the entrance to an underwater village.

30

CHAPTER 5

Tyler raised his hand to indicate '*Take things slowly*'.

Danny nodded and the two of them cruised carefully downwards.

They looked around to make sure they were on their own, and then swam through the archway.

As they carried on, they could see that this strange undersea village was about the same size as their own.

They spied a series of strange buildings that must surely be homes for the merpeople.

They passed a large bare table surrounded by chairs and benches. Was this a place for eating meals?

On they went, swimming past something that looked like a kitchen. There were plates, knives and spoons, all made of some strange, hard material so they didn't float away.

But there was no food in sight.

There were no merpeople in sight either. This undersea kingdom seemed to be completely deserted.

Danny suddenly raised his arm and they both stopped.

There, on the ground at the start of a track, was a purple and red shoe. Tyler picked it up and turned it over in his hands.

It was one of the mayor's shoes.

At the same time, Danny noticed a flurry of movement behind them.

Danny and Tyler spun round and were horrified to see a large group of menacing-looking merpeople swimming incredibly quickly and heading straight in their direction.

CHAPTER 6

Turning to their right, Danny and Tyler swam along another trail. They swam faster than they'd ever swum before.

In and out of shacks they turned, the army of merpeople behind them, making a fearsome sight.

Swerving round stone pillars, Danny's heart raced like a bullet train. What would the merpeople do to them if they caught them? Would they kill them?

Had they already killed the mayor?

As he frantically forced his arms and legs to move, swimming as hard as he could, Danny quickly calculated how much oxygen they had left. It had to be at least twenty-five minutes.

Didn't it?

Tyler indicated left and Danny followed him. They swam past a small shed. Its door was open and, looking in, they could see it was some kind of store room.

Danny could see the merpeople getting closer, and it felt like they would reach Danny and Tyler any second. Fighting off two mermen had been tough enough; dealing with a whole army would be impossible.

Danny's arms were starting to ache, but he knew he couldn't let up, even for a second.

Taking a sharp right turn, Danny looked up and his heart sank. He and Tyler had entered a dead-end passage with a roof over it.

They swam towards the wall at the far end and swam up to the roof. They pushed at it but it didn't budge.

They had no options.

The merpeople would be on them in seconds.

Chapter 7

They waited for the attack, but watched in amazement as the merpeople swam straight past the dead-end passage, thinking they were still on the right path to catch the humans.

After waiting for a few minutes, Danny and Tyler swam back to the entrance of the passage and peered out. There was no sign of the merpeople.

Quickly they retraced their steps to the place where they'd found the mayor's shoe.

They carried on, following the trail, and quite soon they found the mayor's other shoe.

They swam on and found the flower he always wore in the buttonhole of his jacket.

Danny and Tyler stuck to the trail and a little further on discovered his wallet.

A short way further along the trail they stopped in front of a large black building. The white front door was open.

Tyler put a finger to his lips and they snuck inside.

They swam along a corridor with pictures of various merpeople on the walls. They spotted another door, this one blue.

Swimming through it, they found themselves in a large square room.

There was only one thing in the room.

A large steel cage.

And inside the cage was the mayor.

CHAPTER 8

Danny stared at the mayor in shock.

He was wearing some kind of jerkin with a cape and wore a facemask that allowed him to breathe underwater.

But how could the merpeople do this? Locking him up in a cage!

And why?

The mayor was overjoyed to see Danny and Tyler. He waved his hands around wildly, pointing at something.

Danny scanned the room and finally spotted a key hanging on a hook on the wall.

Retrieving the key, Danny hurried to the cage and quickly unlocked the door. The mayor jumped out. Relief and joy were all over his face.

'Quick,' said the mayor through his facemask. 'We need to get out of here as quickly as possible. Those merpeople are going to KILL me!'

Danny was shocked. Suddenly he could hear what the mayor was saying.

'Wait!' said Tyler.

Danny could hear Tyler, too. Obviously the merpeople had some way of enabling everybody to understand each other underwater.

The mayor spoke again. 'I said, those merpeople are going to KILL me! We must leave!'

Danny frowned.

Why would the merpeople kill the mayor if they were holding him to ransom? Didn't they want to exchange him for gold coins?

'MOVE!' commanded the mayor.

As they turned to leave, a merman wearing a large gold crown swam into the room.

This had to be the merpeople's king. And he had come for them.

Before Danny could even think, the mayor grabbed a long piece of metal off the floor and raised it above his head.

Instantly he brought the metal crashing down towards the merman king's skull.

CHAPTER 9

Danny acted instantly. He knocked the metal out of the mayor's hands.

'WHAT ARE YOU DOING?' screamed the mayor.

'You can't just go around killing people!' mouthed Danny.

'But these merpeople are going to kill ME!' snapped the mayor. 'I TOLD YOU!'

The merman king looked at the mayor in amazement.

'Kill you?' he asked in shock. 'You know we're not going to kill you!'

'Let's get out of here!' said the mayor frantically.

'No!' said Tyler. 'I want to hear what the merman king has to say for himself.'

'I really think we should … ' tried the mayor again, but Danny shot him a look and he fell silent.

'What's going on?' demanded Tyler.

The merman king sighed as he started his story.

'For many years we have traded gold with your mayor in return for food,' explained the merman king. 'But then our gold ran out.'

'So you have known about these merpeople all the time!' said Tyler, looking at the mayor.

'I … I … I … ' said the mayor, but Tyler shushed him.

'The mayor said he would give us NOTHING until we found more gold,' said the king. 'We tried, but we couldn't find any. All of our gold had been given to the mayor.'

'So how are you eating at the moment?' asked Tyler.

'We're not,' replied the merman king wearily.

'So the mayor left you down here to starve?' said Danny. He thought of the empty kitchen, the storeroom and the bare table.

The merman king nodded. 'We had to solve the problem, or we would all perish. In desperation we kidnapped the mayor. We couldn't think of anything else to do.'

'So you and your fellow merpeople aren't evil at all,' mouthed Tyler in astonishment.

'Those two mermen who attacked us did so because you all needed to hold onto the mayor so that you could eat again!'

'Correct,' nodded the merman king.

'I'm out of here!' screamed the mayor.

He barged past the merman king, Danny and Tyler, and sprang out of the room.

CHAPTER 10

Danny grabbed the mayor by the leg and pulled him back.

Keeping a beady eye on him, Danny, Tyler and the merman king thrashed out a plan that would benefit everyone – the mermen under water and the humans on land.

The king then called all the merpeople together and they assembled outside.

The king explained to his people what had been decided, and the plan was accepted.

The two mermen who'd attacked Danny and Tyler on the way down apologised and Danny and Tyler said it was fine – they understood now why it had happened.

All through these talks the mayor stood sheepishly to the side.

*****

Only minutes later, with less than one minute's oxygen left, Danny, Tyler, the merman king and the mayor surfaced.

Danny, Tyler and the mayor climbed into the boat. The king preferred to swim alongside.

*****

The entire village was waiting for them when they reached the shore. Someone had spotted Danny and Tyler setting out that morning and had told everyone that they were up to something.

Caleb was the first to greet them.

'I am so sorry for not believing your stories,' he said to Tyler, looking at the merman king in amazement. 'I should have listened.'

Caleb and the others bowed low to the merman king, who explained to the crowd what the mayor had been doing. There were shouts of anger.

'You were going to starve them!' cried someone with rage.

'We have solved the problem,' said Tyler, raising his hand for quiet. 'We will provide the merpeople with all of the food they need.'

People nodded their agreement.

'And in return they will allow us to take tour groups of people to see their undersea village,' said Danny.

'That way we will earn some money for the village, which will help us provide food for our new undersea friends.'

'Brilliant idea!' shouted someone.

'And ... ' said Tyler, 'We've chosen a first class tour guide. '

'A man who will wear a special uniform and show all of the tourists round,' added Danny.

'Is it you?' called out somebody.

'No,' grinned Danny. 'It's the mayor!'

There were roars of approval.

'Everybody wins!' continued Danny. 'We help the merpeople and get some money, the merpeople get all the food they need and the mayor gets the chance to learn to respect other people.'

Everyone cheered and clapped.

Except, that is, for the mayor.

Mermaids

The word 'mermaid' comes from the Old English word for sea ('mere'), and 'maid' which is a girl or young woman.

The first mermaid stories were written around 3,000 years ago in a country called Assyria.

The original story was about a beautiful goddess who fell in love with a shepherd and accidentally killed him! She was so ashamed that she jumped into a lake and turned into a fish to try and hide. But even the water couldn't hide her beauty. So she kept her mermaid tail, but changed back to being human above the waist.

In some stories, mermaids help sailors in times of trouble, rescuing those lost at sea.

In other stories, mermaids sing enchanting songs and lure sailors to dangerous waters – where they are then shipwrecked on rocks.

Mermen

We don't know very much about mermen.

In old Irish stories, mermen were very ugly creatures.

In ancient Greek stories, mermen often had beards and hair like seaweed.

Mermen from Finland were magical and handsome and could help to cure illnesses.

THE LOST CITY OF ATLANTIS

Is there really a lost city under the sea? Is it called Atlantis?

Thousands of years ago the Greek writer Plato wrote about a beautiful city, built on an island called Atlantis. It was ruined overnight by a flood.

Some people have said that this city really existed. If we keep looking, they say, we will find it.

Many books and films have been based on this idea of a perfect, magical city, lost beneath the waves.

*Now read the first chapter of another great
Toxic title by Jonny Zucker:*

ISLAND SHOCK

Chapter 1

Mike Chen woke up with a start.

He opened his eyes slowly and had to hold up his hand to protect them from a glaring light.

The last thing he remembered was falling asleep at the airport terminal, where he'd been waiting to catch a plane.

He lowered his hand and was astonished by the sight that greeted him.

He was on a beach.

Sand stretched all around him. Gentle waters from a vast ocean lapped onto the shore. A couple of huge trees bearing strange orange fruit stood a short distance away on the sand.

There was no sign of Mac or Robbie, or any of the other kids from school who'd been waiting with him for the plane to France.

What on Earth was going on? Where was he – and how had he got here?

He scanned the ground for his rucksack. He couldn't see it.

Maybe Mr Masters had tricked them all, and instead of going to France he'd taken them to some remote island.

But if that was true, where were the others?

'MAC! ROBBIE! MR MASTERS!' he called.

Nothing. Just the sound of the sea.

Scratching his head in total bewilderment, Mike stood up and looked behind him.

A jungle of trees, bushes and wild grass lay before him, stretching into the distance as far as he could see.

It looked like he was on an island – one of those desert islands you sometimes see in the movies.

But it was impossible to tell from here how big the island was. It might be no more than a hundred metres. It might be thirty times that size.

Mike realised he was incredibly thirsty. He walked towards the trees and saw a small rock pool, fed by a tiny stream.

Crouching down, he cupped his hands and dipped them into the pool. Drinking from his hands, he was pleased to find that the water wasn't salty.

At least he had fresh water.

He had just splashed some water on his face when he heard a thumping sound a short way away.

He turned quickly to his right, but all he saw was the sea gently rolling up onto the beach.

But when he turned to his left his heart froze.

Snaking its way out of the jungle next to the sea, and whacking its tail on the ground, was a large, scaly, terrifying-looking crocodile.

MORE GREAT TOXIC READS

Action-packed adventure stories featuring jungles, swamps, deserted islands, robots, space travel, zombies, computer viruses and monsters from the deep.

How many have you read?

JONNY ZUCKER

FOOTBALL FORCE

by Jonny Zucker

It's 2066 and football has changed. Players now wear lightweight body armour. Logan Smith wants to play for the best local team – Vestige United. Their players are fantastic, but Logan suspects that the team has a dark secret.

MORE GREAT TOXIC READS

ISLAND SHOCK

by Jonny Zucker

Mike Chen wakes up on a deserted beach. The last thing he remembers is waiting for a flight at the airport. How did he get here? Where are his friends? Mike soon realises that he is surrounded by danger on all sides. Can he survive the attacks of wild creatures and find out what is going on?

GLADIATOR REVIVAL

by Jonny Zucker

Nick and Kat are on holiday in Rome with their parents. So how do they end up facing the perils of the Coliseum in ancient Rome – as gladiators? Is somebody making a film? Or is this for real and they are fighting for their lives?

Crash Land Earth

by Jonny Zucker

Jed and his friends are setting out on a trip to Mars. But their spaceship is in trouble and they are forced to crash-land back on Earth. But nothing is quite as it should be. Jed and his fellow explorers find themselves in a race against time to save planet Earth.

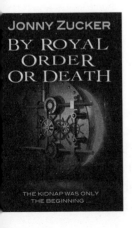

By Royal Order or Death

by Jonny Zucker

Miles is a member of the Royal Protection Hub, whose job is to protect the Royal family. When Princess Helena is kidnapped, Miles uncovers a cunning and dangerous plot. Miles must use all his skills to outwit the kidnappers and save the princess's life.

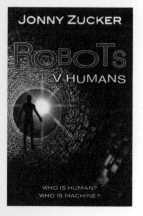

ROBOTS V HUMANS

by Jonny Zucker

Nico finds himself with five other kids – all his age. None of them can remember anything from their past. Then they are told that three of them are human and the other three are robots. Can Nico find out who is human and who are the robots?

ZOMBIE CAMP

by Jonny Zucker

Arjun and Kev are at summer camp. It's great – there's lots to do and places to explore. But after a while Arjun and Kev begin to suspect that nothing is quite as it seems. Can they avoid the terrible fate that awaits them?

MORE GREAT TOXIC READS

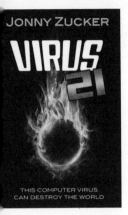

JONNY ZUCKER

VIRUS 21

by Jonny Zucker

A new computer virus is rapidly spreading throughout the world. It is infecting everything, closing down hospitals, airports and even the internet. Can Troy and Macy find the hackers before the whole world shuts down?

JOHN TOWNSEND

TERROR OF THE SWAMP

by John Townsend

Ex-SAS explorer Baron and his son Greg have been sent to the African jungle to find a lost TV crew. It's a search that brings them face to face with the mysterious ancient terrors of the swamp – and it could cost them their lives.

Jonny Zucker has been a teacher, musician, stand-up comedian and footballer, but now he is best known as one of the most popular authors for children. So far he has written over 100 books.

Jonny also plays in a band and has done over 60 gigs as a stand-up comedian, reaching the London Region Final of the BBC New Comedy awards.

He still dreams of being a professional footballer.